5/2/07 Penworthy $17.96

JUSTICE LEAGUE UNLIMITED

united
they stand

Written by:
Adam Beechen

Colored by:
Heroic Age

Illustrated by:
Carlo Barberi
Ethen Beavers
Walden Wong

Lettered by:
Phil Balsman
Pat Brosseau
Nick J. Napolitano

Superman created by **Jerry Siegel** and **Joe Shuster**

Batman created by **Bob Kane**

Wonder Woman created by **William Moulton Marston**

JUSTICE LEAGUE UNLIMITED VOL. 1: UNITED THEY STAND
Published by DC Comics. Cover and compilation copyright © 2005 DC Comics.
All Rights Reserved. Originally published in single magazine form as JUSTICE
LEAGUE UNLIMITED 1-5. Copyright © 2004, 2005 DC Comics. All Rights Reserved.
All characters, their distinctive likenesses and related elements featured in this
publication are trademarks of DC Comics. The stories, characters and incidents
featured in this publication are entirely fictional. DC Comics does not read
or accept unsolicited submissions of ideas, stories or artwork.

CARTOON NETWORK and its logo are trademarks of Cartoon Network.

DC Comics, 1700 Broadway, New York, NY 10019
A Warner Bros. Entertainment Company.
Printed in Canada. Second Printing.
ISBN: 1-4012-0512-7. ISBN 13: 978-1-4012-0512-6.
Publication design by John J. Hill.

WB SHIELD ™ & © Warner Bros. Entertainment Inc.
(s05)

3

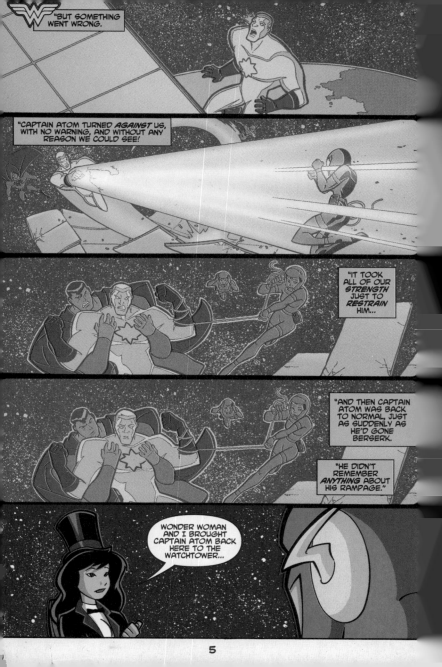

"BUT SOMETHING WENT WRONG.

"CAPTAIN ATOM TURNED *AGAINST* US, WITH NO WARNING, AND WITHOUT ANY REASON WE COULD SEE!

"IT TOOK ALL OF OUR *STRENGTH* JUST TO *RESTRAIN* HIM...

"AND THEN CAPTAIN ATOM WAS BACK TO NORMAL, JUST AS SUDDENLY AS HE'D GONE BERSERK.

"HE DIDN'T REMEMBER *ANYTHING* ABOUT HIS RAMPAGE."

WONDER WOMAN AND I BROUGHT CAPTAIN ATOM BACK HERE TO THE WATCHTOWER...

"LUCKILY, WONDER WOMAN RETURNED TO NORMAL BEFORE ANY SERIOUS DAMAGE WAS DONE."

"AS BEFORE, WE COULD FIND NO CAUSE FOR HER RAMPAGE."

BUT THE *WORST* WAS YET TO COME.

"WHILE WONDER WOMAN AND ZATANNA WERE ATTENDING TO CAPTAIN ATOM, I HAD RETURNED TO THE SPACE STATION'S MISSION CONTROL TO TELL THEM WE'D REPAIRED THE DAMAGE DONE."

"WHAT HAPPENED NEXT WAS TOLD TO ME LATER, BECAUSE I HAVE NO MEMORY OF IT..."

"IT LASTED FOR HALF AN HOUR. THREE OF THE MIGHTIEST BEINGS ALIVE, TURNED INTO FORCES OF DESTRUCTION."

"AND WHEN IT WAS OVER...

"...ALL WE COULD DO WAS BE GRATEFUL IT HADN'T BEEN *WORSE*."

WE RAN ALL THE SAME TESTS ON SUPERMAN THAT WE RAN ON WONDER WOMAN AND ME, BUT WE DIDN'T REALLY EXPECT TO FIND ANYTHING...

...AND WE *DIDN'T*.

THERE'S SOMETHING ABOUT THIS I DON'T GET...

WHATEVER IT WAS THAT HAPPENED ONLY AFFECTED CAPTAIN ATOM, WONDER WOMAN, AND SUPERMAN...

...BUT ZATANNA WAS THERE FOR EACH RAMPAGE, TOO!

WHY WEREN'T *YOU* AFFECTED, Z?

WE WONDERED THE SAME THING. WE RAN TESTS ON ME, TO SEE IF THERE WERE ANY UNUSUAL READINGS, OR IF I WAS SOMEHOW THE CAUSE OF THE OTHERS' PROBLEMS.

WE COULDN'T FIND ANYTHING.

I THINK THE REASON WHY ZATANNA WASN'T AFFECTED IS FAIRLY OBVIOUS, FLASH...

SHE'S NOT AS PHYSICALLY POWERFUL AS THE OTHERS.

NO KIDDING...

NONE OF *US* ARE. AND NONE OF US WERE TARGETED.

TARGETED? BATMAN, WHAT ARE YOU TRYING TO SAY?

I'M SAYING, HAWKGIRL, THAT THERE WERE FOUR DIFFERENT JUSTICE LEAGUERS, IN DIFFERENT COMBINATIONS, PRESENT DURING ALL THE... *"SPELLS,"* IF YOU'LL PARDON THE TERM.

THE FIRST THREE *"SPELLS"* AFFECTED THE STRONGEST THREE JUSTICE LEAGUE MEMBERS. THE FOURTH SPELL AFFECTED ALL THREE AT THE SAME TIME, BUT *NOT* ZATANNA.

CAPTAIN ATOM, SUPERMAN AND WONDER WOMAN ALL HAVE RADICALLY DIFFERENT PHYSIOLOGIES, SO IT'S DOUBTFUL THAT ANY ILLNESS THAT WOULD AFFECT THE THREE OF THEM WOULDN'T AFFECT ZATANNA, TOO.

IF THREE OF THE STRONGEST BEINGS ON EARTH CAN BE POSSESSED WITH MINDLESS, VIOLENT IMPULSES AT ANY TIME...

THEN WE'RE A DANGER TO THE ENTIRE WORLD... AND EVERYONE ON IT.

THEREFORE, WE'RE GETTING AS FAR AWAY FROM POPULATED AREAS, AND EACH OTHER... AS POSSIBLE. AT LEAST UNTIL OUR "SEIZURES" STOP HAPPENING, OR WE FIND A WAY TO CURE THEM.

I'VE LOCATED A DESERTED ASTEROID 4.7 LIGHT-YEARS AWAY. I'M HEADED THERE.

SUPERMAN HAS ALLOWED ME TO STAY AT HIS ARCTIC FORTRESS OF SOLITUDE.

I'M HEADED TO THE SOUTH POLE.

IT'S REALLY THE ONLY CHOICE WE HAVE.

14

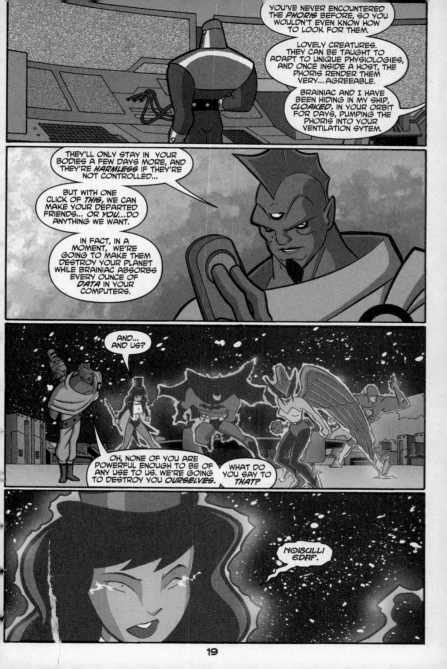

19

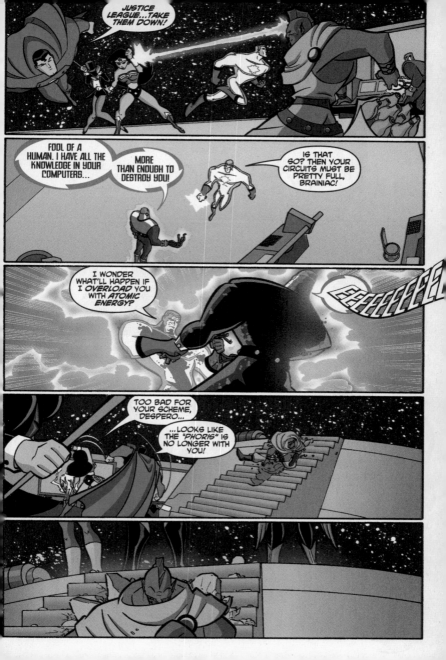

24

25

31

34

LUTHOR'S HAIRPIECE! I WIN *AGAIN!*

BOOSTER, I WAS *BLUFFING!* I CAN'T *BELIEVE* YOU FOLDED A *FULL HOUSE!* WHAT WERE YOU *THINKING?*

HEY, *TEAMWORK...* THAT'S WHAT THE JUSTICE LEAGUE IS ALL ABOUT.

HUH?

NEVER MIND, SUPERMAN... JUST *DEAL.*

END.

45

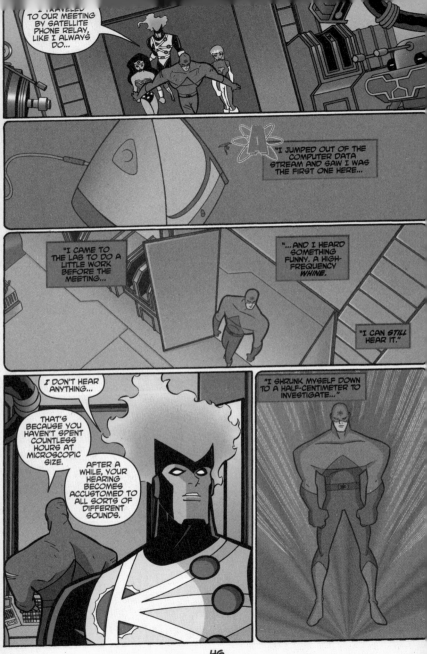

TO OUR MEETING BY SATELLITE PHONE RELAY, LIKE I ALWAYS DO...

"I JUMPED OUT OF THE COMPUTER DATA STREAM AND SAW I WAS THE FIRST ONE HERE...

"I CAME TO THE LAB TO DO A LITTLE WORK BEFORE THE MEETING...

"...AND I HEARD SOMETHING FUNNY. A HIGH-FREQUENCY *WHINE.*

"I CAN *STILL* HEAR IT."

I DON'T HEAR ANYTHING...

THAT'S BECAUSE YOU HAVEN'T SPENT COUNTLESS HOURS AT MICROSCOPIC SIZE.

AFTER A WHILE, YOUR HEARING BECOMES ACCUSTOMED TO ALL SORTS OF DIFFERENT SOUNDS.

"I SHRUNK MYSELF DOWN TO A HALF-CENTIMETER TO INVESTIGATE..."

WHO, ATOM? WHO *ARE* THEY?

THEY'RE *COLONIZERS*, WONDER WOMAN...

...AN OTHER-DIMENSIONAL *ARMY!*

"I SAW MILLIONS OF THEM THROUGH THE RIFT...*BILLIONS*... JUST WAITING TO COME THROUGH..."

"THE *FIRST* WAVE OF INVADERS KEPT ME OCCUPIED AS THE SECOND WAVE STARTED CONSTRUCTING A *DEVICE* OF SORTS..."

"I ASSUME TO *WIDEN* THE RIFT SO THE ENTIRE ARMY COULD COME THROUGH!"

"I BARELY ESCAPED... I KNEW I HAD TO GET HELP..."

"IF THE INVADERS GET THAT PROJECTOR SET UP AND WIDEN THE RIFT, THERE'LL BE TOO MANY OF THEM TO STOP...*EVER*."

UM, THIS MIGHT BE A STUPID QUESTION, BUT...

...COULDN'T WE JUST, YOU KNOW, *STEP* ON THEM?

OR USE THE PHANTOM ZONE THINGIE TO *POOF* 'EM AND THEIR STUFF AWAY?

48

TO SEAL AN INTERDIMENSIONAL RIFT?

BECAUSE *I* DON'T. WE'RE GOING TO NEED THEIR EQUIPMENT.

STUPID QUESTION.

THANKS.

OKAY, WE'RE READY.

READY FOR WHAT?

THANKS TO THIS MACHINE, THESE DEVICES WILL RECEIVE THE SIGNALS FROM MY BELT CONTROLLER THAT ALLOW ME TO SHRINK AND GROW.

ONCE WE'RE ALL DOWN TO SIZE, WE CAN TAKE THE BATTLE TO THE INVADERS!

NOW, YOU'VE ALL BEEN SHRUNK DOWN BEFORE, RIGHT?

WONDERFUL. GREAT. WELL, THERE'S NO TIME TO TRAIN YOU FOR YOUR FIRST SHRINK, SO I'LL JUST HAVE TO FILL YOU IN ON THE LITTLE THINGS AS WE GO ALONG.

FIRST LESSON: WHEN YOU START SHRINKING, BLOW OUT ALL THE BREATH YOU HAVE.

HOW COME?

BECAUSE YOUR LUNGS ARE GOING TO SHRINK WITH THE REST OF YOU, AND IF THERE'S A LOT OF AIR IN THERE WHEN THEY START GETTING SMALLER...

...BOOM.

BIG EXHALE. RIGHT. GOT IT.

CHECK.

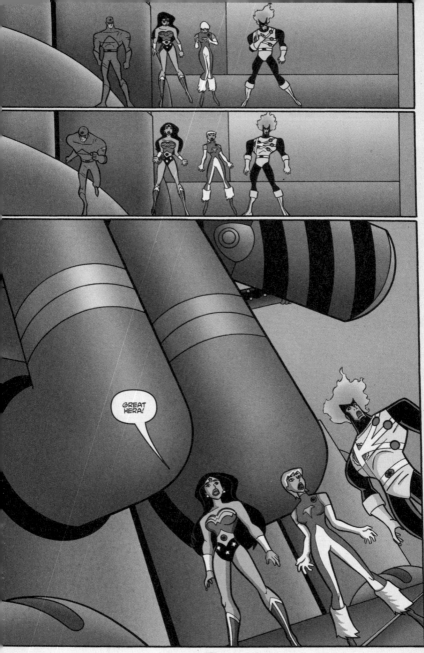

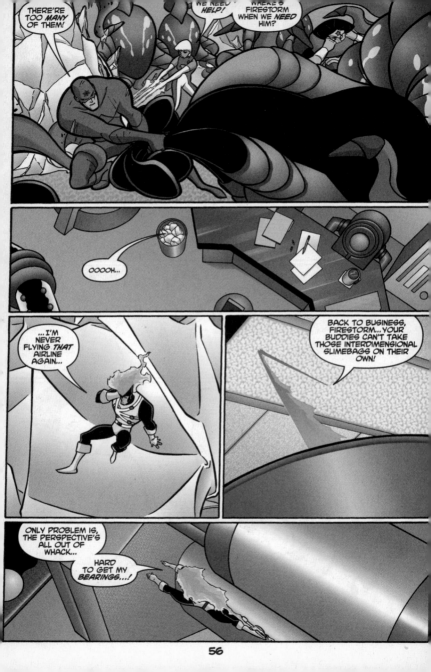

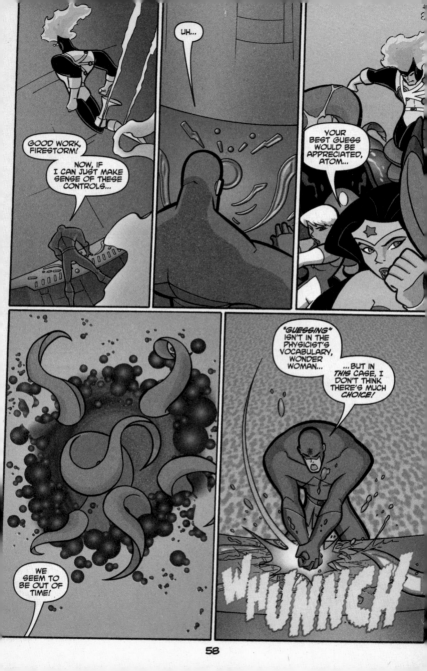

I HAVE SEEN THE PEOPLE OF EARTH TREAT *SUPERMAN* THIS WAY...

...BUT HE IS *SUPERMAN.*

SARDATH... THE CITIZENS OF RANN DO THIS *OFTEN?*

EVERY TIME HE SAVES THE PLANET, YES...

FROM THE MOMENT HE WAS ACCIDENTALLY BROUGHT HERE BY MY EXPERIMENTAL *ZETA BEAM,* ADAM STRANGE HAS BEEN OUR *PROTECTOR.*

"TIME AND AGAIN, HE HAS PUT THE SAFETY OF RANN BEFORE HIS OWN SAFETY, TO COMBAT INTERSTELLAR INVADERS AND NATURAL DISASTERS--

"NO RANNIAN IS MORE FORTUNATE THAN I THAT ADAM HAS CHOSEN TO MAKE RANN HIS HOME RATHER THAN RETURN TO EARTH...

"SOMETIMES WITH YOUR ASSISTANCE, LIKE TODAY.

"...FOR HE IS HUSBAND TO MY DAUGHTER ALANNA, AND FATHER TO MY GRANDDAUGHTER, ALEEA."

I WONDER...

EARTH, *MY* ADOPTED PLANET, IS *CROWDED* WITH HEROES, LIKE MY FELLOW JUSTICE LEAGUE MEMBERS.

WHILE A FEW HEROES, LIKE SUPERMAN AND MYSELF, ARE FROM OTHER WORLDS....

...MOST OTHERS, LIKE BATMAN, WERE BORN ON EARTH AND HAVE CHOSEN TO SPEND THEIR LIVES PROTECTING IT.

WE ARE THERE TO FIGHT THE MENACES NORMAL HUMANS CANNOT.

EARTH HAS *MANY* HEROES BORN ON ITS SOIL...

...WHERE ARE RANN'S OWN?

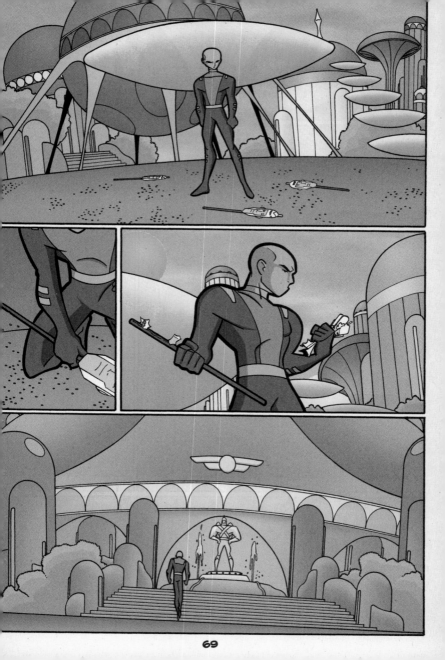

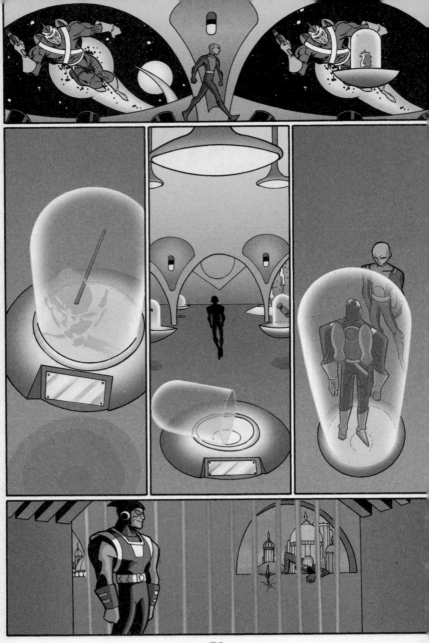

DO I THINK ABOUT MOVING BACK TO EARTH?

NEVER.

BUT IT IS THE PLANET OF YOUR BIRTH. DO YOU NOT MISS IT? I MISS MARS AT EVERY MOMENT.

ADAM AND HIS FAMILY TRAVEL TO EARTH BY ZETA BEAM TO VISIT ALL THE TIME.

ELONGATED MAN IS RIGHT, BUT I DO MISS EARTH, MANHUNTER. ALTHOUGH, NOW RANN FEELS LIKE *HOME* TO ME.

MY DAUGHTER WAS *BORN* HERE. MY WIFE'S FAMILY IS *FROM* HERE...

ON EARTH, I'M JUST ANOTHER GUY.

WHEN I CAME *HERE,* I FOUND THE IMPORTANT THINGS...

...ON RANN, I'M *NEEDED.*

GOOB!

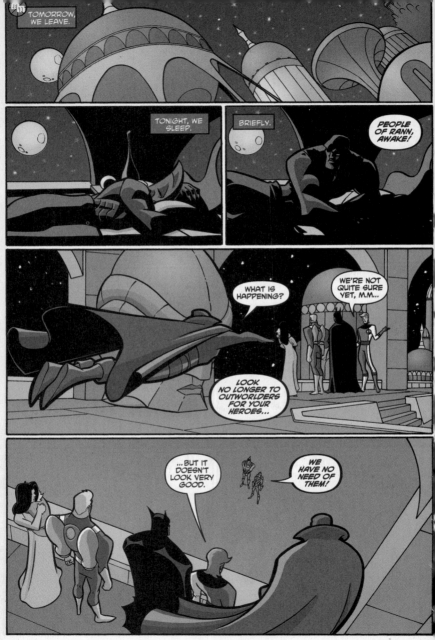

73

75

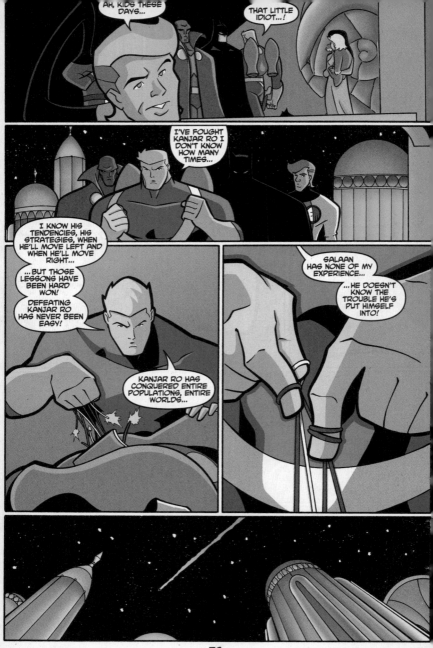

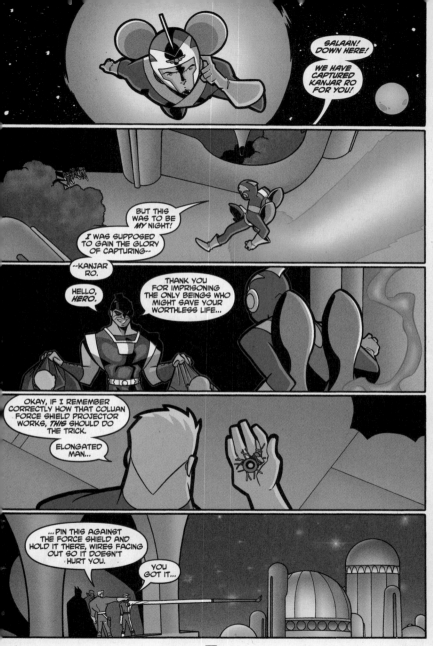

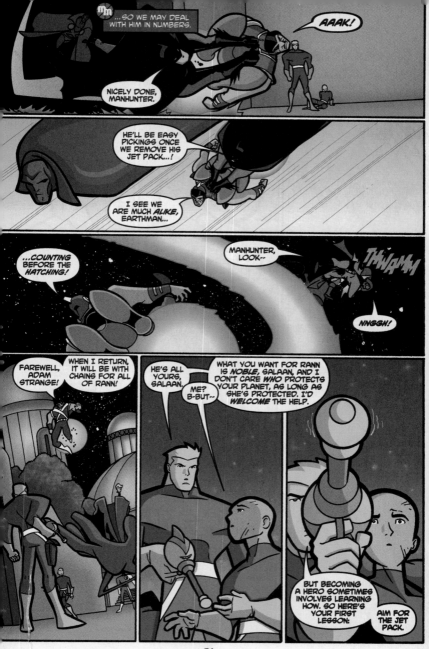

...SO WE MAY DEAL WITH HIM IN NUMBERS.

AAAK!

NICELY DONE, MANHUNTER.

HE'LL BE EASY PICKINGS ONCE WE REMOVE HIS JET PACK...!

I SEE WE ARE MUCH *ALIKE*, EARTHMAN...

...COUNTING BEFORE THE HATCHING!

MANHUNTER, LOOK--

THWAMM

NNGGH!

FAREWELL, ADAM STRANGE!

WHEN I RETURN, IT WILL BE WITH CHAINS FOR ALL OF RANN!

HE'S ALL YOURS, SALAAN.

ME? B-BUT--

WHAT YOU WANT FOR RANN IS *NOBLE*, SALAAN, AND I DON'T CARE *WHO* PROTECTS YOUR PLANET, AS LONG AS SHE'S PROTECTED. I'D *WELCOME* THE HELP.

BUT BECOMING A HERO SOMETIMES INVOLVES LEARNING HOW. SO HERE'S YOUR FIRST LESSON:

AIM FOR THE JET PACK.

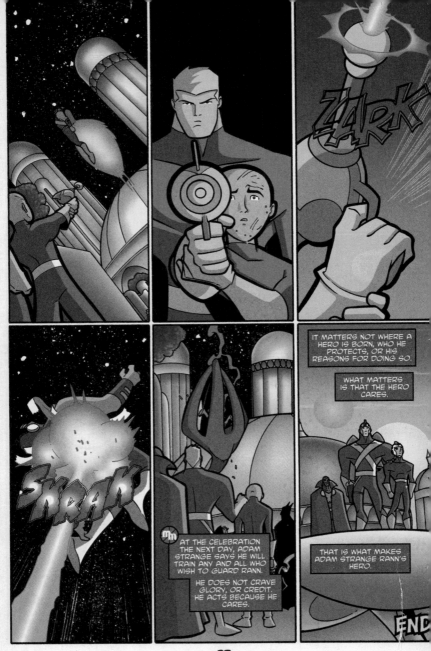

ZZARK

SHRAK

AT THE CELEBRATION THE NEXT DAY, ADAM STRANGE SAYS HE WILL TRAIN ANY AND ALL WHO WISH TO GUARD RANN.

HE DOES NOT CRAVE GLORY, OR CREDIT. HE ACTS BECAUSE HE CARES.

IT MATTERS NOT WHERE A HERO IS BORN, WHO HE PROTECTS, OR HIS REASONS FOR DOING SO.

WHAT MATTERS IS THAT THE HERO CARES.

THAT IS WHAT MAKES ADAM STRANGE RANN'S HERO.

END

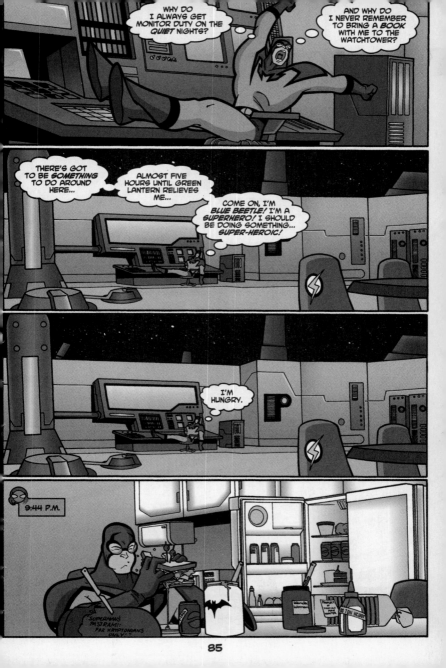

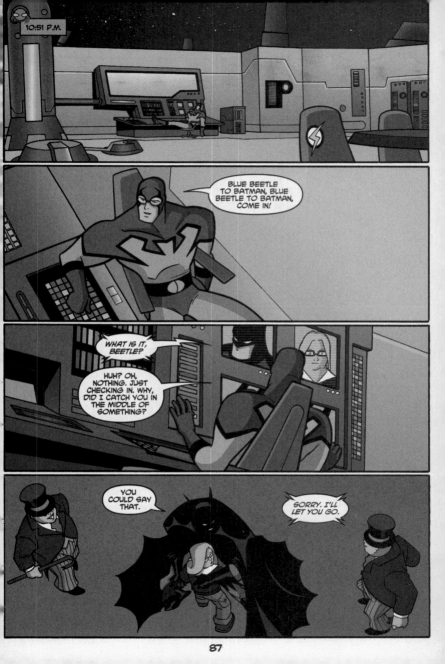

87

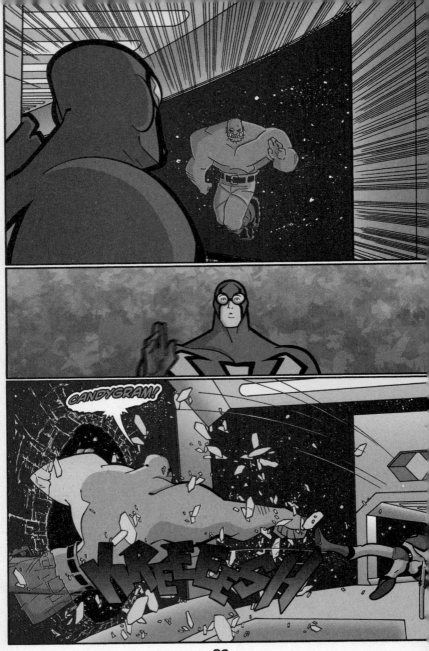

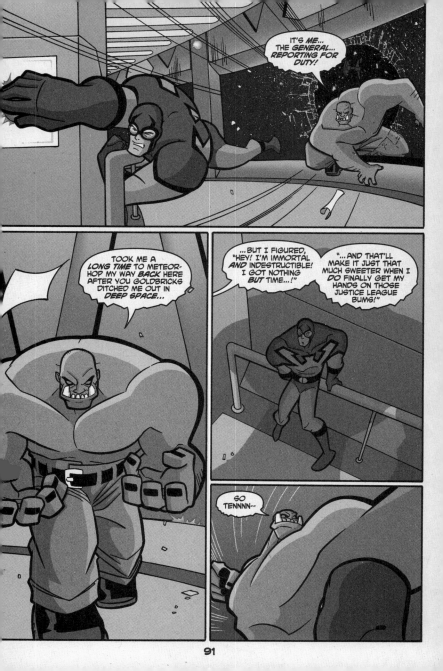

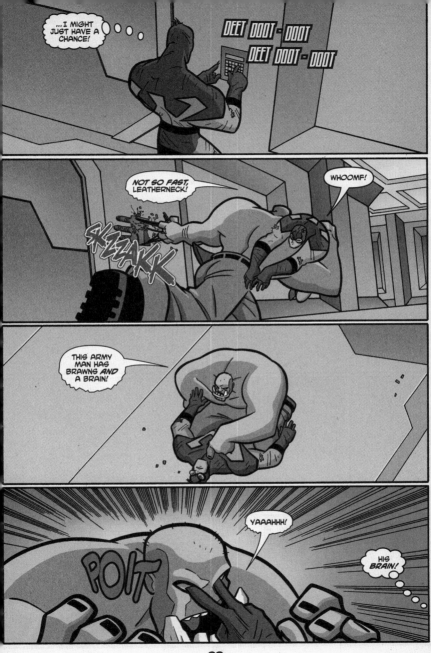

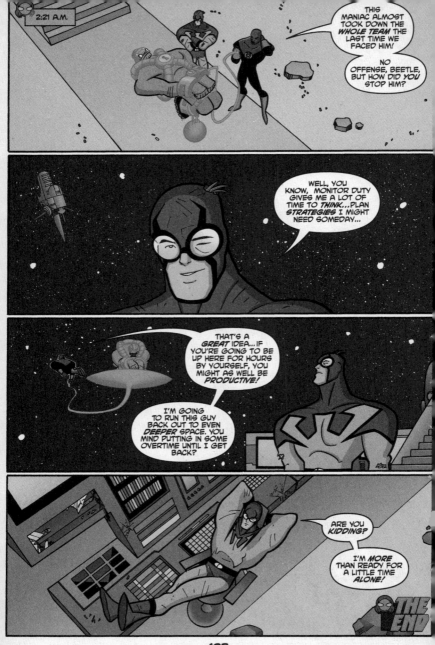